Happy 3rd Birthday
Emme!

Love,
    Steffi × Craig

Dream BiG, PRINCESS!

Aurora • Merida • Tiana
Snow White • Cinderella • Ariel
POCAHONTAS • Rapunzel
Mulan • Belle • JASMINE

ISBN 978-0-7364-3709-7
randomhousekids.com
Printed in the United States of America
10 9 8 7 6 5 4 3 2 1

Dream BIG, PRINCESS!

By Andrea Posner-Sanchez · Designed by Megan McLaughlin

Random House  New York

Being a princess is easier than you might think.

...and
REACH
for the
SKY!

Be a friend to all.

Look after those smaller
than you.

Be a
DEEP THINKER...

. . . and a GOOD LISTENER.

WORK HARD.

Be open to **MEETING** <u>new</u> **PEOPLE**...

...and trying
NEW THINGS.

Don't get
discouraged
if you hit
a bump in
the road.

IF YOU FALL,
PICK YOURSELF
RIGHT BACK UP.

Try looking at things
from a different angle.

DON'T JUDGE a BOOK BY ITS COVER.

Always
SEE the
GOOD in
others.

BE UNIQUE.

It's okay to stand out in a crowd.

Know that if you work hard,
all your dreams are within reach.

Exciting opportunities are just outside your door.

you CAN CONQUER the WORLD!

SO TAKE YOUR BEST SHOT.

Be STRONG and FACE your FEARS.

Find your
inner
WARRIOR.

Remember—
IT'S OKAY to
ask for HELP
IF YOU NEED IT.

Be brave.

Embrace change.

JUMP INTO NEW ADVENTURES.

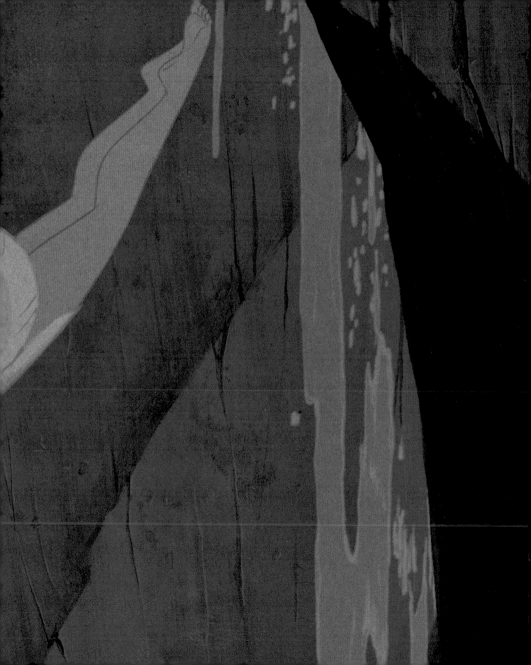

Always be kind.

And celebrate
what a great
princess
you are.

DANCE!

Climb high!

GET CREATIVE!

Go for a ride!

Release your inner ROCK STAR!

Never stop learning.

NEVER STOP EXPLORING.

and NEVER STOP
DREAMING!